小龍嗡嗡嗡

Lucy Kincaid 著

Eric Kincaid 繪

陳韋倩 譯

三民書局

The Little Dragon   ISBN 1 85854 777 6
Written by Lucy Kincaid and illustrated by Eric Kincaid
First published in 1998
Under the title The Little Dragon
by Brimax Books Limited
4/5 Studlands Park Ind. Estate,
Newmarket, Suffolk, CB8 7AU

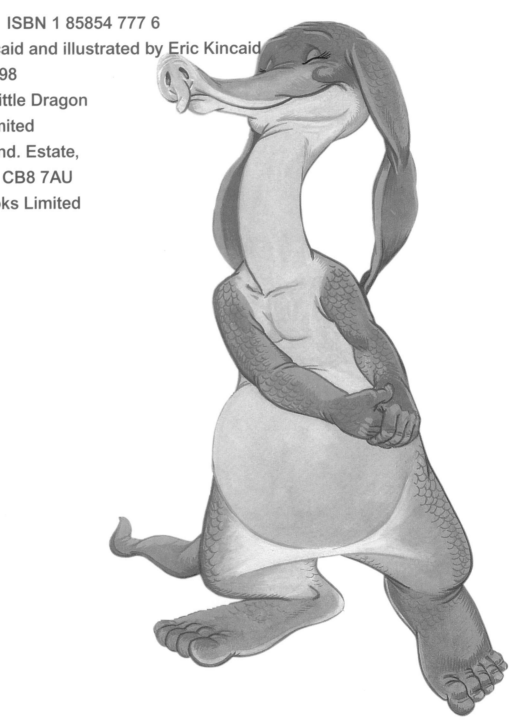

小龍和貓頭鷹

Little Dragon and Sleepy Owl

Little Dragon has many friends in the wood. Owl is one of them.
Owl is **awake** all night and **sleeps** during the day.
Little Dragon **waves** to Owl as he **flies** home.

awake [ə`wek]
形 醒的

sleep [slip]
動 睡覺

wave [wev]
動 揮（手）

fly [flaɪ]
動 飛

小龍在樹林裡擁有許多的朋友，
貓頭鷹其中的一個。
貓頭鷹整個晚上都醒著，白天才
呼呼大睡。
在貓頭鷹飛回家的途中，小龍向
他揮了揮手。

But Owl is not happy.
All the animals want to **talk** to him
during the day. Owl is very tired. He
cannot work day and night. He
must get some sleep.
Owl goes to see Little Dragon.

talk [tɔk]
働 講話

可是貓頭鷹一點也不高興！
在白天的時候，所有的動物都想
和他聊天。貓頭鷹累壞了。他沒法
兒白天和晚上都工作呀！他得要
好好睡個覺。
貓頭鷹便去找小龍。

"**W**ill you **stand under** my tree?" says Owl. "Then no one will come to talk to me. I must get some sleep."

"I will help you sleep," says Little Dragon.

So Owl goes back to his tree and Little Dragon stands under it.

stand [stænd]
動 站

under [ˋʌndɚ]
介 在…下面

「你能站在我的樹下嗎？」貓頭鷹說。「那樣就不會有人來和我聊天了。我必須好好睡個覺！」
「我會幫你睡好覺的。」小龍說。
於是貓頭鷹回到了樹上，小龍就站在樹底下。

A mouse comes to see Owl. Little Dragon **growls**. The mouse runs away.

A **squirrel** comes to see Owl. Little Dragon growls. The squirrel runs away.

Little Dragon growls when anyone comes near the tree.

mouse [maʊs]
名 老鼠

growl [graʊl]
動 怒吼

squirrel [ˋskwɝˑəl]
名 松鼠

一隻小老鼠來拜訪貓頭鷹。小龍怒吼了一聲，小老鼠便跑掉了。
一隻小松鼠來拜訪貓頭鷹。小龍怒吼了一聲，小松鼠便跑掉了。
一有人靠近這棵樹，小龍就會大聲吼叫。

"Are you **asleep**, Owl?" asks Little Dragon.
"No," says Owl.
"Why not?" asks Little Dragon.
"Your growls keep me awake," says Owl.
"I'm sorry," says Little Dragon.
"What can I do?"

asleep [əˋslip]
形 睡著的

「你睡著了嗎，貓頭鷹？」小龍問。
「沒有啊！」貓頭鷹說。
「為什麼沒有呀？」小龍問。
「你的吼叫聲讓我睡不著呀！」貓頭鷹說。
「對不起啦！」小龍說。「那我該怎麼做呢？」

The bees know what to do. They know a sleeping song.

"Hum hum hum," hum the bees.

"**Close** your eyes. Go to sleep."

"Hum hum hum." Little Dragon hums too. "Close your eyes. Go to sleep. Hum hum hum."

close [kloz]
動 閉

蜜蜂們知道怎麼辦。他們知道一首安眠曲。

「嗡嗡嗡！」蜜蜂們嗡嗡嗡地哼著。

「閉起眼睛，快快睡吧！」

「嗡嗡嗡！」小龍也嗡嗡嗡地哼著。

「閉起眼睛，快快睡吧！嗡嗡嗡！」

Owl's eyes are shut. Owl is asleep.

"Do not stop humming," say the birds. "Owl will **wake up** if you do." Little Dragon **keeps on** humming. So do the bees.

wake [wek]
動 醒

wake up
醒來

keep on
繼續

貓頭鷹閉起眼睛，睡著了呢！
「繼續嗡嗡叫，別停喲！」鳥兒們說。「如果停了下來，貓頭鷹就會醒過來的。」
小龍便繼續哼著。蜜蜂們也是。

The animals listen to the song.
They get **sleepy**.
The birds listen to the song. They
get sleepy.
Soon they are all asleep.

sleepy [`slipɪ]
形 想睡的

soon [sun]
副 不久

動物們聽著聽著，漸漸地想睡覺了。
鳥兒們聽著聽著，也想睡覺了。
一會兒，他們全睡著了。

HM-MM-M

HM-MM-MM-M-MM

HM-MMMMM-M-M

M-M-MM-M-MM-M-M-M

The bees are awake. The bees are still humming.

Little Dragon is still awake. He is still humming.

The bees are getting sleepy.

Little Dragon puts his **paws** over his ears.

paw [pɔ]
名 掌

蜜蜂們是醒著的，他們還一直嗡嗡嗡地哼著。

小龍仍然醒著，他也還一直嗡嗡嗡呢！

蜜蜂們越來越想睡覺。

小龍用手掌搗住了自己的耳朵。

The bees are asleep.
Little Dragon is still wide awake.
His paws are over his ears. Little
Dragon cannot hear the sleeping
song.

蜜ㄇㄧˋ蜂ㄈㄥ們ㄇㄣ˙睡ㄕㄨㄟˋ著ㄓㄠ˙了ㄌㄜ˙。
小ㄒㄧㄠˇ龍ㄌㄨㄥˊ可ㄎㄜˇ還ㄏㄞˊ清ㄑㄧㄥ醒ㄒㄧㄥˇ得ㄉㄜ˙很ㄏㄣˇ呢ㄋㄜ˙！
他ㄊㄚ用ㄩㄥˋ手ㄕㄡˇ掌ㄓㄤˇ摀ㄨˇ住ㄓㄨˋ耳ㄦˇ朵ㄉㄨㄛ˙，便ㄅㄧㄢˋ聽ㄊㄧㄥ不ㄅㄨˊ見ㄐㄧㄢˋ這ㄓㄜˋ
首ㄕㄡˇ安ㄢ眠ㄇㄧㄢˊ曲ㄑㄩˇ了ㄌㄜ˙。

Owl wakes up.

"I cannot hear anyone," says Owl.

Little Dragon tells him they are all asleep.

Owl **laughs** when he sees everyone. He laughs so much that everyone wakes up. And then they all laugh too.

laugh [læf]
動 笑

貓頭鷹醒了。

「我聽不見其他人的聲音呢！」貓頭鷹說。

小龍告訴他大夥兒全睡著了。

當貓頭鷹看見大夥兒的模樣，大笑了起來。他笑得好大聲喲！把大夥兒吵醒了，然後他們也全都笑了起來。

23

小普羅藝術叢書

《我喜歡》系列

《創意小畫

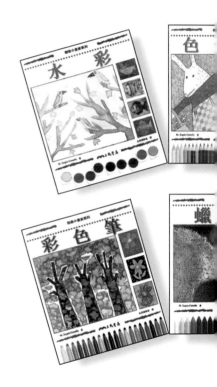

《創意小畫家

《聯合報》讀書

由西班牙 *Parramón ediciones, s. a.* 獨家授權出版

24×30cm／精裝／15冊

》系列

《小畫家的天空》系列

當一個天才小畫家
發揮想像力
讓色彩和線條在紙上跳起舞來！！

教你怎麼用面紙拼貼、畫各種風景、
動物，還有冰淇淋哦！！

列 榮獲

最佳童書

我愛阿瑟系列

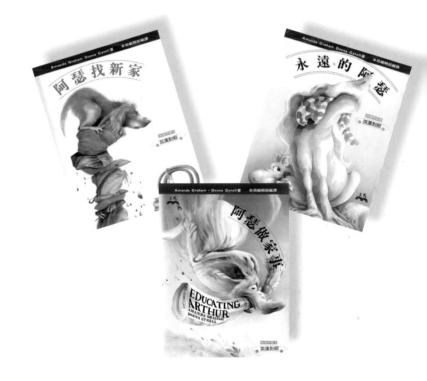

I LOVE ARTHUR

Amanda Graham・Donna Gynell著　本局編輯部編譯

20×27cm／精裝／3冊／30頁

阿瑟是一隻不起眼的小黃狗，為了討主人歡心，他什麼都願意做，但是，天啊！為什麼他就是一天到晚惹麻煩呢！？

一連三集，酷狗阿瑟搏命演出，要你笑得滿地找牙！

他練習游泳、吐氣泡，還有在水中呼吸，
他很努力地練習著，直到他確信，
自己可以當條金魚。
（摘自《阿瑟找新家》）

網際網路位址　http : // www. sanmin. com. tw

© 小龍和貓頭鷹

著作人　Lucy Kincaid
繪圖者　Eric Kincaid
譯　者　陳韋倩
發行人　劉振強
著作財　三民書局股份有限公司
產權人
　　　　臺北市復興北路三八六號
發行所　三民書局股份有限公司
　　　　地址／臺北市復興北路三八六號
　　　　電話／二五〇〇六〇〇
　　　　郵撥／〇〇〇九九九八———五號
印刷所　三民書局股份有限公司
門市部　復北店／臺北市復興北路三八六號
　　　　重南店／臺北市重慶南路一段六十一號
初　版　中華民國八十八年十一月
編　號　S85523
定　價　新臺幣壹佰捌拾元整
行政院新聞局登記證局版臺業字第〇二〇〇號

有著作權，不准侵害

ISBN　957-14-3081-1（精裝）